Farmer Doogie

Farmer Doogie

Peter Curry

Collins

An imprint of HarperCollins*Publishers*

What does Farmer Doogie do?

MOO

He collects all the eggs.

Then what does Farmer Doogie do?

He counts up all his sheep.

Then what does Farmer Doogie do?

He picks lots of apples.

He opens his little shop.

Oh, no! The tractor's broken down!

Now what does Farmer Doogie do?

He has to get
his tractor book...

...and his big box of tools...

...so he can mend the tractor!

Now what does Farmer Doogie do?

He fetches some old clothes...

...and makes a jolly scarecrow!

That's what Farmer Doogie does!

First published in Great Britain by HarperCollins*Publishers* Ltd in 2001

1 3 5 7 9 10 8 6 4 2

ISBN: 0-00-664741 3

The HarperCollins website address is:
www.fireandwater.com

Printed in Singapore by Imago

GAYLORD M

Also by Peter Curry:

Meet *Nosy Rosy* the little anteater who just can't help poking her big nose into other people's business!

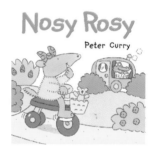

Learn to count from 1-10 with *Ten Sleepy Bunnies* and a host of other animals.

And for babies and toddlers look out for the irresistible *All Aboard* board books.

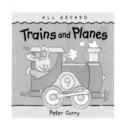
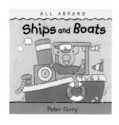
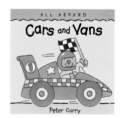
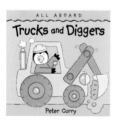